An ,

this story cracks
me up! I hope

CHRISTMAS WITH SAINT

❄

you enjoy it

by

J. Sterling

xux J.St.

CHRISTMAS WITH SAINT

Copyright © 2022 by J. Sterling

All Rights Reserved

Edited by:

Jovana Shirley

Unforeseen Editing

www.unforeseenediting.com

Cover Design by:

Michelle Preast

www.Michelle-Preast.com

www.facebook.com/IndieBookCovers

ISBN:

978-1-945042-51-5

No part of this book may be reproduced or transmitted in any form or by any means, electronic or mechanical, including photocopying, recording, or by any information storage and retrieval system without the written permission of the author, except for the use of brief quotations in a book review.

This is a work of fiction. Names, characters, businesses, places, events, and incidents are either the products of the author's imagination or used in a fictitious manner. Any resemblance to actual persons, living or dead, or actual events is purely coincidental.

Please visit the author's website
www.j-sterling.com
to find out where additional versions may be purchased.

Other Books by J. Sterling

Bitter Rivals—an enemies-to-lovers romance

Dear Heart, I Hate You

In Dreams—a new adult college romance

Chance Encounters—a coming-of-age story

THE GAME SERIES

The Perfect Game—Book One

The Game Changer—Book Two

The Sweetest Game—Book Three

The Other Game (Dean Carter)—Book Four

THE PLAYBOY SERIAL

Avoiding the Playboy—Episode #1

Resisting the Playboy—Episode #2

Wanting the Playboy—Episode #3

THE CELEBRITY SERIES

Seeing Stars—Madison & Walker

Breaking Stars—Paige & Tatum

Losing Stars—Quinn & Ryson

THE FISHER BROTHERS SERIES

No Bad Days—a new adult, second-chance romance

Guy Hater—an emotional love story

Adios Pantalones—a single-mom romance

Happy Ending

SANTA'S FAVORITE ELF

IVY

"**Y**OU'VE GOT TO be kidding me," I said as I tugged at the flimsy material attempting to cover my ass. "This thing is way too short. I can't wear this."

I looked at my best friend, Cori, whose expression was torn between comical and concerned as her violet-colored bob swished around with her movements. "You look hot."

She was the only person I knew who could not only pull off that haircut, but also any color she decided to change it to. Cori was as experimental with her hair as I was safe. No one touched these golden locks, except me.

Narrowing my eyes, I glanced down at my exposed thighs once more. "I'm not supposed to look hot. I'm one of Santa's elves!"

"Yeah, the hot one," she mumbled under her breath,

and I almost lunged for her, but I knew it would rip the so-called skirt in half. Or at least bust the zipper. "Ivy, it's fine," she said, trying to placate me.

"It's not fine." I pulled at the material, trying in vain to make it rest on my hips instead of my waist so I could get a little more length out of it. "This event is for kids, not their dads."

"Who do you think brings them here?" she asked, and I realized that she'd planned for this. All of this.

"Cori, I'm not going out there in this. I can't even bend over. I'm sure elves have to bend at some point."

"Put some Spanx on underneath then. That way, when you move around, you won't be showing your goodies to all the horny dads out there." She glanced at the watch on her wrist. "Where is he?" She was talking to herself as she looked around the otherwise empty room.

"Who's playing Santa this year anyway?" I asked right as Saint freaking LaCroix walked through the dressing room doors, carrying a pair of black boots, his blue eyes sparkling, even in the fluorescent lighting.

"Ho ho ho! I am." His voice sent chills down my spine and made my thighs quiver. He sucked all the air out of the room the minute he waltzed into it.

Trying to pull it together, I shot Cori a murderous glare that let her know she could have at least warned me. But then that wouldn't have been any fun ... *for her*. Instead, I spun around and practically hopped into Saint's arms as he wrapped himself around me, making my skirt go all the way up. I felt the cool breeze of air on my exposed ass cheeks as I breathed in his scent.

I had no idea what he wore that made him smell so good, but it always caused a visceral reaction in me. It was like it'd imprinted on me at some point, become a part of my DNA or some kind of sensory memory. One time, when I had been walking through the mall, the same smell drifted past me, and I almost fell to my knees in response. Whipping my head around, I'd searched for Saint, but he was nowhere to be found.

"Santa would never get any work done if you were at the North Pole," he whispered into my ear, and I smacked his shoulder as I hopped down and adjusted my clothes.

I'd been pathetically in love with Saint since I had come out of the womb. At least that was how it always felt because I couldn't remember a time when I didn't have it bad for him. He'd always been sweet about it, subtly flirting back with me and making me feel special instead of embarrassed, but I knew he was just being kind. Saint never looked at me as anything more than his best friend's little sister. Even when I'd started to grow boobs, his eyes had stayed firmly rooted to my own.

It was annoying.

Every other guy stared at my chest instead of my eyeballs, but not Saint. Even when I'd tried to torture him in high school by wearing cleavage-baring crop tops and tank tops so tight that you couldn't help but notice what was hiding behind the fabric, he never even glanced down. There were times I wanted to shove my boobs in his face, but my brother, Davey, would have killed me on the spot. Davey had made it abundantly clear that I was to stay away from his friend. Not that I listened.

The worst part was that Saint knew I was obsessed with him. I'd never been any good at hiding it. And if I'd thought that my feelings could be filed away as some sort of silly schoolgirl crush when I got older, I was sorely mistaken. Saint was still the object of all of my fantasies, even now that we were grown adults. Everything I always liked about him had grown tenfold as he aged.

Why couldn't I just get over him already?

"How did Cori rope you into this one?" I asked, trying to play it cool but I was dying inside.

I'd be spending all day by his side. Five hours of one-on-one time with the only guy I'd ever wanted to kiss, but never had. There was one time when I'd thought it might happen when we were in high school, but he'd ducked away at the last second, and I was too mortified to ever try again.

Now that we were older and had full-time jobs, we didn't see each other as much as we used to when we were kids, but we still kept in touch on social media almost daily, sending each other private messages and silly pictures. Although Saint never looked silly. He always looked downright edible with his messy, dark hair and deep blue eyes.

He and Davey had started a locals-only dating app for the *successful individual*. That was how they marketed it. You had to make a certain income amount to even be accepted onto the site. And each user had to be referred by someone who was already on it.

The whole technical side of things was convoluted and confusing, but I understood at least that much about how it worked. Davey and his fiancée, Samantha, had met on the site, but as far as I knew, Saint wasn't on it. It was a point of contention between him and my brother. Davey was always trying to get Saint to sign up, but Saint refused, saying they already had one owner who was a success story and one was all they needed.

I couldn't have agreed more.

That man needed to never sign up for any dating site. Ever. And if I found out that he did, I would be signing up the next day.

Saint flashed me his trademark smile, the one that made his dimples appear, and I berated myself for all the dirty things I imagined doing to that perfect, chiseled face.

"She asked," was all he said in response to my question. The one I'd completely forgotten asking.

"Get changed, Saint. They're getting antsy out there." Cori appeared between us, shoving a Santa costume into his arms. "Here." She tossed me a pair of black shorts.

"You gonna put those on?" Saint asked with a still-dimpled grin, and I stuck out my tongue. "Seems like a waste if you ask me."

"If I don't, every man out there is going to see my ass every time I move around," I answered, and his face suddenly twisted into an expression I couldn't read.

He looked ... *jealous* instead of his usual irritated glare.

Could that even be possible?

THIS WOMAN

SAINT

*D*EAR *GOD*.

When Ivy mentioned the idea of every guy out there seeing her ass when she moved, I almost came undone. No one who wasn't me should get the privilege of seeing any naked part of her. The woman was a goddess. An absolutely fucking beautiful female who I'd had a crush on for years. A crush I was never allowed to give in to—otherwise, her brother would kill me in my sleep.

He'd threatened it on more than one occasion.

And honestly, since I was always sleeping over at their house, I believed him.

If I didn't have anything to lose, I would have told him to screw himself and gone for it. That Ivy was worth it all.

But Davey and his family had been there for me since

my mom had taken off without warning in the fifth grade, leaving me and my dad alone. My dad worked a lot after that, and if it wasn't for the Simpson family, I would have been by myself, getting into who knew what kind of trouble.

They took me under their wing and treated me like I was one of their own. When Davey and I were younger, Ivy was always following us around, batting her eyelashes up at me like some lovestruck puppy dog. It used to annoy me, and I would call her names in some weak attempt to make her go away. What could I say? I was young and stupid.

But then Ivy grew up. And I did too. And the last thing I felt about her was annoyance. I wanted her to follow me around then. Wished that she would "accidentally" walk into the bathroom just as I was walking out of it. I would have given anything to have her body pressed up against mine when we were teenagers. There had been more than one occasion when we happened to be alone that I thought she might actually kiss me. I would have let her; I would have given in to those lips being pressed against mine as my tongue moved inside her mouth and memorized the way she tasted. I tried to give her all the permission she needed with my body language, but she never followed through. And I couldn't be the one to initiate it, no matter how badly my dick begged me to.

So, I screwed other girls in some pathetic attempt to stop thinking about Ivy. News flash: it didn't work.

I'd never forget the night I got caught checking her out in the living room. She was leaving for a date, and I was so fucking jealous that I couldn't see straight. I stumbled on my words when I tried to give her advice, everything coming out in a jumbled mess that didn't make a lick of sense. And when she walked out the front door with a confused look on her face, I couldn't stop staring at her ass, wishing it were me she was leaving with.

Davey punched me then. Hard. Told me if I didn't stop ogling his little sister, he'd make me leave, and I'd never be welcomed back. Then, he took it one step further and made me promise that I'd never touch her. *Ever.*

"Even when we're thirty," he'd said for clarification.

When I agreed to the request, I knew even then that I was lying, but the thought of being kicked out of the Simpson house terrified me for a multitude of reasons. Not seeing Ivy definitely topped it. Somewhere during our childhood years, she'd become the thing I looked forward to the most. If I didn't get to see her at all, it felt like my whole day was ruined. Like something vital was missing.

And now, here we were—me dressed up like Santa and her as one hell of a sexy elf—and all I could think about was bending her over and sliding her panties to the side, so I could enter her from behind. Her long blonde hair was pulled into a tight ponytail, and she was wearing a pointy green hat. She looked adorable. It was embarrassing how much I still wanted her after all this time.

Even more embarrassing was Davey's continual hold over me about it. We were in some sort of sick and twisted stalemate of who could resist the longest before breaking. Would Davey finally relent and give me his blessing to rail his baby sister? Or would I be the one who gave up on the dream and called it quits once and for all?

Even thinking about letting go made my stomach twist into knots.

Give up on having Ivy?

Not a fucking chance.

Living the rest of my life without tasting her wasn't

something I would ever willingly walk away from. I'd be holding on to that dream until I took my last breath. I'd rather die first.

"Who knew Santa could be so sexy?" Ivy was standing next to me, straightening my beard and fixing my jacket, her green eyes penetrating mine.

"You're just being nice. No one looks sexy in this," I teased, hoping she'd tell me all the ways in which my self-deprecating opinion was wrong.

Her tongue snaked out, and I practically salivated as I watched it move across her bottom lip. Did she need more moisture on her mouth? I'd gladly give it to her. My eyes zeroed in, my dick twitching inside of my Santa pants.

"You put on those shorts, right?" I asked out of nowhere, and she lifted up her skirt to reveal a pair of skintight shorty shorts hidden underneath. "Jesus, Ivy." My voice sounded like I was scolding her, but she'd caught me by surprise by raising it up. My brain almost short-circuited at the thought of what I might get the pleasure of seeing.

"You don't have to get so mad. They're on, okay? You can tell Davey I was a good girl," she said, her tone snarky, and I knew she was irritated. I couldn't even blame her.

"I'm not telling Davey shit." I wanted her to know we weren't kids anymore and the last thing I was doing was reporting back to her big brother about her behavior.

"Yeah right," she argued under her breath, and I took a possessive step toward her, my frame hovering over hers.

"You're a grown woman who can take care of herself and make her own decisions. It's time your brother finally figures that out." I stared into her green eyes, the color of them piercing, rooting me firmly in place. It took every ounce of willpower I possessed to not lean down and give in to what I'd wanted for so long.

"He'll never stop treating me like I'm fifteen," she tried to say, but her voice stuttered, and I wondered if my being this close made her uncomfortable.

Did she still want me as much as she used to?

I wrapped one arm around her waist and pulled her toward me, pieces of her body brushing against parts of mine. "Do I make you nervous, Ivy?"

That damn tongue reappeared once more, licking her top lip this time, and I started shaking my head.

"Put that tongue back in your mouth," I chastised, and she did as I'd asked, which surprised me. I'd figured she'd argue.

"Maybe one day, you'll start seeing me for who I am too." She wiggled out of my grasp and walked out of view, that skirt barely covering her ass with each step she took.

She thought I still saw a teenage girl when I looked at her, as if that was a bad thing. Ivy had no idea that I'd always been in love with that teenage girl.

PUT SAINT UNDER MY TREE

IVY

WHY COULDN'T I just be a normal person whenever it came to Saint LaCroix? His very existence gave me goose bumps and made my knees weak. But the way he'd just pulled me against him like I belonged to him or was somehow his … well, a man shouldn't be able to do that sort of thing if he didn't mean it.

"You're flushed." Cori was suddenly at my side, her eyes narrowed in on my face. "What happened?"

"Saint," was all I said.

One single word, and she understood completely. Cori and I had been friends since high school. Our moms both worked at the salon that my mom owned. And now, Cori and I worked there too. She knew all about my feelings for Saint—both past and present tense. Not that they'd changed much over the years.

"Why do you think I made you do this?" she asked, and I wasn't sure what she was getting at.

"Huh?"

"I *begged* you to be Santa's elf," she said, emphasizing the word *begged*, as if I needed the reminder.

"And?" I implored her to keep talking.

"And I told Saint you were doing it, and he said yes before I even told him what I needed."

Was she saying what I thought she was saying, or was I interpreting things all wrong?

"So, you're telling me—" I started to put the pieces together, but her impatience cut me off instead.

"I'm telling you that he agreed to be here today because you were going to be here."

I started shaking my head in disagreement. "That can't be true."

Cori had been telling me for years that Saint wanted me as much as I wanted him, but I'd figured that she was wrong. Or at the very least, insane. She was my best friend, so of course she encouraged the notion that my lifelong crush would eventually turn into something more.

It was pretty much a prerequisite of being a girlfriend—supporting the fairy tale. We all wanted it in some way, whether we openly admitted it or not. That movie-worthy love story.

"One day, the two of you will get your shit together and put us all out of our misery. But for now, we have kids to make happy."

I followed her out of the dressing room and onto the normally empty stage that had been transformed into a North Pole wonderland. There was fake snow all over the floor and trees, a red-and-green neon sign with an arrow pointing to the left, and a gold-decorated chair for Santa and the kids to sit on. A photographer was finishing setting up, the flash going off every few seconds before he looked up at Cori and gave her a thumbs-up.

"It looks amazing," I whispered, noticing that she was grinning from ear to ear at her achievements as she looked out at the long line of kids waiting, tugging on their parent's arm.

"Who's ready to meet Santa?" Cori shouted, and the kids all yelled back that they were. "Okay! I'll go get him, and you make sure you have your Christmas wish ready."

The children all looked so excited; it was hard not to feed off their energy. I felt myself smiling wide before I even noticed Saint walking out, waving his hands. The kids started jumping up and down, and it was my job to make sure they visited him one at a time.

I walked the first little girl in line over toward Saint and put her on his knee. My eyes roamed up his body and stopped on his blue irises. He was staring at me, and I suddenly found it unfair that this girl got to sit on his lap. I wanted to be on Saint's lap. Naked. With no kids around.

Swallowing hard, I watched as he interacted with the little girl, asking her what she wanted for Christmas and if she'd been naughty or nice.

The girl giggled. "Nice, Santa. Well, except that one time I pushed Bobby off the monkey bars because he called me four eyes."

She adjusted the pair of glasses sitting on her nose, and Saint said something softly to her that I couldn't quite overhear.

When she wrapped her arms around his neck and hugged him hard, I felt pride surge inside my chest. I didn't even know what he'd said to her, but it must have been exactly what she needed. This man was truly something else. They didn't make guys like Saint, and I'd always known it. It was why even when I'd had boyfriends in the past, I had known they weren't the ones for me. A single phone call from Saint asking me to give him a chance, and I would have dropped each and every one like a hot potato. It wasn't fair of me to keep dating guys who would always be stuck in second place.

Then again, it wasn't fair to me to keep pining over the one guy who wouldn't give me the time of day. If we weren't supposed to be together, then how come I never liked anyone more than I liked him? Why couldn't I see myself with anyone else when I imagined my future?

"Hot elf"—Saint's deep voice hit my ears, and I turned to look at him questioningly—"can you get the next kid?"

"Sorry," I said before returning my focus to the task at hand.

The little girl was already almost out the front door with a candy cane in her hand and a giant smile on her face as she talked animatedly to her mom.

When I bent down to grab the next little boy in line by the hand, I heard an intake of breath that sounded more like a hiss, and I noticed that the kid's dad was staring directly at my ass, his eyes roving the length of my body.

I stood up quickly and made sure my skirt was back in place, attempting to cover everything even though I knew it barely could.

"Here you go," I said to Saint, who was currently shooting daggers from behind his old-man spectacles at the dad who had been eyeing me.

Even behind the white gloves that he wore, I could see his hands gripping the arms of his chair, his fingers digging into the fabric, like he was forcing himself to stay seated instead of getting up and charging like a bull who saw nothing but red.

That was twice today that Saint had acted like a jealous boyfriend. Maybe my Christmas wish was finally coming true. The one I'd written on a separate list since I had been eight.

Would Santa put Saint under my tree this year? I sure as hell hoped so.

TAKING HER HOME

SAINT

THE DOOR SLAMMED as the last child exited the building, and I blew out a long breath, leaning my head against the oversize chair and forcing my eyes to stay open. No one had warned me how exhausting it was, playing a role for five hours straight. The constant smiling, ho ho ho'ing, and being "on" for every man, woman, and child.

"You two were great. Thank you so much for doing that," Cori said, and it made me feel like I'd done something good even though I'd only agreed to do this because I knew Ivy was doing it too.

Selfish? A little.

It had started snowing pretty hard while we were indoors, playing make-believe for the kids. The once-clear windows were now frosted over with ice. The weather here could be dangerous even if you grew up driving in it. Storms were unpredictable and often reminded you who was in charge.

Note: it wasn't you or your car.

"I have to pee. Be right back," Ivy said before disappearing, her skirt swishing from side to side as she jogged toward the bathroom door.

Cori started stacking some of the decorations, putting them into a pile, and I realized that I needed her on my side. A girl's best friend was either your greatest ally or your worst enemy.

"I'll give you twenty bucks if you let me take Ivy home."

Cori's gaze swept to mine, a giant smile on her face. "Twenty bucks?" She stood up tall and put her hand on her hip, like that amount of money wasn't nearly enough to buy her as my co-conspirator.

"Fifty," I countered, and she gave me an easy nod.

"I'll take fifty."

"And you'll help me out," I pushed, hoping she was picking up what I was silently putting down.

"You mean, encourage my bestie to go home with you? To be alone in a car with the only guy she's ever wanted? Yeah, I'm sure that will be a tough sell."

I must have made some sort of surprised face because she called me out instantly. "Don't give me that look." She pointed her finger at my face. "You know she's always been in love with you. Everyone knows."

The sound of Ivy's shoes shuffling against the tiled floor had us instantly quieting down. Cori looked at me and gestured throwing dollar bills out of her palm like she was at a strip club. Little did she know that I would have paid her a hundred.

"What are you two up to?" Ivy asked as soon as she neared.

"I was telling Cori that I'm going to drive you home," I informed instead of asking, and she looked at her best friend before looking back at me.

"Whyyyyy?" she said, dragging out the word.

"I noticed your car wasn't outside. And the weather's shit."

"Are you saying I'm a bad driver?" Cori interjected, and I should have known she was going to throw a wrench into my plans. "That I can't get our girl home in one piece? I'm offended."

Ivy started nodding her head in agreement. "I think he is saying that, Cor. Pretty rude."

The two of them were making this difficult, but I was up for the challenge.

"So, you don't want me to take you home?" I decided to use a different approach and put Ivy on the spot. If she refused to let me drive her, she was going to have to say out loud that she didn't want it ... *that she didn't want me.*

Her cheeks instantly started to turn pink. "I didn't say that. It's just that Cori and I had plans after. Right?" She widened her eyes, silently asking Cori to go along with the obvious lie.

Enough games.

Enough wasted time.

My body suddenly felt like it might waste away and die if I spent another second without her underneath me. I'd been denying my true feelings for years. I couldn't do it anymore. I was irrational and consumed with lust.

"You two don't have plans. And honestly, I don't care if you do. Cancel them," I said sternly, and Cori pressed her lips together to stop from either laughing or talking—I wasn't sure which.

"Or what?" Ivy pushed, her long legs on full display. "You'll call my brother and rat me out?"

Her brother. Everything about us always came back to him. Not tonight. Not right now.

"Good God, Ivy. My car's full. Can't fit you," Cori said, and I smiled, letting her know she'd earned that fifty.

"Your car isn't full. I rode here in it," Ivy argued.

"I have to put all these decorations somewhere." Cori waved a hand toward the decor that was in no way going inside anyone's car. They stayed here in a storage closet, and we all knew it.

"Fine, Saint. You can take me home, I guess. Let me go change," she said, but I reached for her arm and held her still.

"Don't get out of that outfit." I'd been imagining all the things I could do to her in that tiny little skirt. The last thing I wanted was her out of it. We were going to play Santa and the naughty elf if I got my way.

"Hey," Cori complained, "you can't keep the clothes."

"We can for one night," I suggested.

Cori rubbed her fingers together in the air, hinting that it would cost me. I gave her a nod.

Ivy looked down at her outfit before looking at mine. "You're staying in the Santa suit?"

"I'm staying in the Santa suit."

She shrugged. "You're being really weird, but I'm here for it."

I could tell that Ivy had no idea what I was planning or hoping would happen after we got to her place. We'd been friends for so long that she trusted me enough to simply go along with whatever I requested, no questions asked. It was one of the things I loved most about us—the fact that friendship was the base of our foundation. And in my opinion, nothing was stronger than that.

THE DRIVE BACK to her apartment on the lake was relatively quiet. I remembered when she'd scored the place. She'd been so excited while the rest of us were seething with jealousy. It had been a hell of a deal through an old family friend who didn't want to sell it, but wasn't ever going to live there again. There were too many stairs, and it was too loud on the weekends with all the tourists. Bars and restaurants lined the street. Not to mention, all of the boats and pontoons docked right underneath her balcony. The location was grade A, and Ivy jumped at the chance. She hosted parties all the time in the summer, but I hadn't been here in almost a year, and I was instantly regretting it. how work was always getting in the way.

I glanced over at Ivy, who I could tell wasn't quite sure what I was up to and she was far too nervous to ask. What if my answer wasn't what she wanted to hear? At least, that was what I assumed. Christmas music played in the background, and I turned it down a little with the button on my steering wheel.

"Are you okay? Is your seat heater working?"

I wanted her to be comfortable even though we'd never done anything as simple as this before. Driving together in a car should be an everyday occurrence for people who were old friends, but for me and Ivy, it just wasn't. We'd been in cars often, but never alone. And never lately.

"It's nice," she said as she scooted her back into it. "This is nice," she added, and I wanted to reach out and put my hand on her thigh.

I could tell there was more going on in that gorgeous head of hers, but she wasn't saying any of it out loud.

"Ivy," I breathed out as I focused on the road and the snow falling, not saying anything else even though I had a million thoughts racing in my head.

"Saint ..." She said my name in response, waiting. "Is my family at my place? Is that why we're still in these clothes?"

I laughed, glancing at her for only a second before watching my headlights illuminate the trees. "No. No one's there."

"Then, why'd you make me stay in this?"

I gave myself a quick pep talk and decided that I had nothing to lose. I'd already come this far, and I planned on taking it a hell of a lot further once we got to her place. "Because I've been fantasizing about you in it all day. Do you have any idea how sexy you look? How hard it was for me to focus on the kids and not your ass for five hours?"

She sucked in an audible breath before she started whispering things I couldn't quite make out. I noticed that she pinched her arm.

"Is this real?"

"It's real," I answered, and her mouth dropped open slightly, like she hadn't meant for me to hear the question, let alone answer it.

"How, Saint? Why now?"

"Because I can't wait anymore."

HE WANTS ME?

IVY

H E COULDN'T WAIT anymore? *HE couldn't wait anymore?*

I'd been waiting a million years for this man to look at me like he wanted me, and now, he was telling me that he did? For how long? Since when?

I had so many questions and zero answers.

It was a crazy feeling though—getting the one thing you wanted after so many years of pining for it. It was almost unnatural. Like it couldn't really be happening. Saint had always been just out of reach, and a part of me had figured he'd always stay that way. Wanting him, but not having him was a notion I'd grown comfortable with.

And now that he was telling me differently, I was anything but comfortable.

"Did I say something wrong?" His voice broke through the carols on the radio and the pounding of my heart.

"No. You just caught me off guard," I admitted, shifting in my seat. It was suddenly too hot. Or maybe I was sweating.

"In a good way?" he asked as we pulled onto the gravel road that led to my lakeside apartment.

The snow had left a blanket of white on the ground and in the tree branches. Everything looked so pretty and peaceful. It was Christmastime at its finest.

I ignored his question completely and reached for my purse, so I could attempt to fish out my keys. My fingers were shaking, and I did my best to hide that from Saint as he put his car in park, but didn't shut off the engine.

"Are you coming inside?" I asked as I continued the search, shaking my purse and hearing the sound of keys clanging, but not seeing them anywhere.

His hand was suddenly on my arm, his fingertips squeezing my skin, demanding my attention. I swallowed hard, trying not to focus on how his touch sent chills down every part of my skin.

"Ivy, look at me."

I did as he'd asked. Hell, I couldn't remember a time when I didn't acquiesce to his every request.

"Are you coming in or not?" I asked again, this time facing him and looking right into his eyes, daring him to follow through on all the things he'd said in the car ride over.

"If you'll let me."

A loud, "*HA*," escaped from deep within my throat because that statement had to be a joke. This man knew I'd let him do anything he wanted.

"If I find my keys," I complained, and he reached for my purse, taking it out of my lap and checking the side pocket before pulling them free.

"Found 'em," he said with a smug look and an arrogant half-smile.

My brain kept screaming at me that we were finally going to kiss Saint LaCroix. What if he was bad at it? I almost giggled out loud. That wasn't allowed to be a possibility, so I told my brain to shush.

I hopped out of the warmth of his car and into the freezing air. The wind whipped my skirt around, and I almost cursed him for making me wear this while he was bundled up in layers of Santa gear.

The sound of the locks engaging on his car hit my ears right before his horn beeped once.

"Let's get you inside." He was suddenly at my side, his arms wrapped around my middle as we rushed toward the entrance.

Once inside the building, he followed me up the long wooden staircase toward my front door. My apartment was on the second level of a two-story structure and had the best views of the lake without being accessible by drunken tourists or locals. Since I lived alone, it felt safer than being on the ground floor.

The long walk up the stairs also gave Saint time to second-guess what he was doing here or talk himself out of doing it. Two things I hoped he didn't give in to. I unlocked and pushed open my front door, and the smell of pine hit my nose. My Christmas tree was in the corner of the living room, the top of it pressing against the ceiling and folding over. I'd been so proud of it when I bought it the other day, determined to make it fit even though it clearly didn't.

"It smells so good in here," Saint said from behind me

as I put my purse down on the countertop in the kitchen.

"It's the tree." I waved a hand toward my tall beauty.

His hand was on my arm again, turning me around to face him. I sucked in a breath with the contact and waited for him to take the lead. Without warning, he was gripping my face between his fingertips, his thumb tracing lines down the side of my cheek and across my bottom lip. I closed my eyes and leaned in to him, craving more.

"I've wanted to do this for years," he said, and my eyes popped open just in time to see him moving in for the kill.

His mouth was on mine, his lips soft and tentative at first before quickly turning into something more demanding and less controlled. His tongue forced its way inside my mouth, and I opened for him, giving him the access that he desired. That kiss was like an inferno, blazing to life with just one strike of the match. So many years of longing exploded between us, and we couldn't seem to keep our hands off each other.

Rough fingers were on my ass, under my skirt, then on my back, pulling my hair out of the ponytail it was in, and then back on my ass again, squeezing me hard enough to leave bruises. It was like he couldn't keep them in one place for too long or they might get stuck there. With every move, however, he never stopped kissing me. Our mouths never broke contact. We were fused together, our tongues touching and pulling back in some kind of dance, our mouths opening and closing as we breathed the same air.

"God, Ivy."

His words were hot against me, and I did the unthinkable and pulled away. It was only to tease him though, and I ran my hands down the length of my body before pulling my shorts and panties off from underneath my skirt and dropping them to the floor.

Saint looked like he might attack me at any moment, his eyes filled with lust as he wiped his mouth with the back of his hand. Was I making this man drool? I sure as hell hoped so. Reaching for the buttons on the elf costume top, I undid them one by one. His jaw slacked open as he finally looked at my boobs spilling out from inside my lace bra instead of my eyes.

It's about time. Only took him a hundred years.

"You'll be the death of me," he said.

I felt spurred on even more with his admission.

Confidence soared through me.

"When did you realize?" I asked, wanting at least that answer before we took this any further.

"Realize what?"

His blue eyes were still focused on parts of my body instead of my face, and I reveled in it. I'd tried so hard as a kid to get him to look at my figure, and now, when I'd given up that game, he couldn't seem to get enough.

"That you had feelings for me," I said before growing uncomfortably nervous, my confidence disappearing as quickly as it had shown up.

Saint never said he had feelings for me.

He'd only said that he wanted me. Sex and actual emotions were two completely different things. I wasn't sure that I could give my body to Saint and carry on like nothing had happened between us. No matter how long I'd yearned for his touch, I knew that it would destroy me to share my bed with him and have him walk away.

"Do you want to talk it all out first?" he asked as he leaned against the counter, and I knew that he was seriously wondering and not mocking me.

Even with the hard bulge sticking out of his ridiculous

Santa pants, he was willing to stuff it down and have a conversation before doing anything more.

I nodded. "I think I need to. I can't do this with you if it means nothing."

And that was the truth. Even though I'd crushed on Saint for as long as I could remember, it had never been just a physical thing for me. He was the whole package. My ideal man. The guy I measured everyone else up against. Someone no one would ever compare to.

If we weren't on the same page, then I had to jump out of the book completely once and for all and never crack open the spine again.

FINALLY COMING CLEAN

SAINT

I VY THOUGHT I didn't have real feelings for her. It was about time to clear the air and come clean. I'd been keeping it all to myself for far too long, too scared to cross the line or break the promise I'd made to Davey all those years ago. I cared about my best friend and didn't want to disappoint him, but staying away from Ivy was denying myself true happiness. Something I knew I'd never find with any other woman ... because they wouldn't ever be her. And trust me, I'd tried. They all ended the same way—with me wishing they were blonde-haired and green-eyed with a sweet smile that was only meant for me and no one else.

"You honestly think this means nothing to me?" I wanted to be offended, but I couldn't be.

The poor woman had no idea how I felt, and how could she? I'd never told her before today.

"I was just asking. I mean, I can't have sex with you if that's all you want from me," she said, and I closed the small space between us and placed my hand on the back of her neck.

"I want you," I said with a kiss, "badly." I kissed her again, my tongue sweeping across her lower lip before taking it in my mouth and moaning. "But it's not just sex for me."

Her entire body relaxed underneath my grasp. Relief seemed to fill her, but in order to give her a little space to breathe, I took a step back. We both stood there in the kitchen, seemingly afraid that if we left this part of the apartment, what we had started would abruptly end.

"Really?" She didn't sound entirely convinced.

"I've wanted to be with you since I was seventeen years old."

There. I'd done it. Laid it all on the line, to hell with the consequences.

I really fucking hope Davey understands and doesn't kill me. Or ruin our company.

"Seventeen?" she asked, and I could see the wheels in her mind spinning as she tried to place where and why I'd said that particular age.

"You were leaving the house for a date with Jordan freaking Ramsey." My lips twisted into a snarl as I said his name, but something inside of her clicked into place. I saw it all over her face.

"I remember."

"You were wearing low-rise jeans and this little white half-shirt. You had on a silver chain that wrapped around your stomach."

"How do you remember that?"

"I remember everything."

She gasped at my response as though she couldn't quite believe it. Like all of this information was too much for her brain to process at once.

"But I went on the date." She shrugged, still trying to make sense of all the things I hadn't told her yet.

"And I was seething with jealousy."

"You were not." She sounded incredulous. "You never even looked at me."

"I looked at you. I noticed you. Every change in your

body. Every outfit you put on. Every time you tried to make my dick hard by wearing practically nothing in front of me and then bending over for no reason."

I felt myself getting worked up, just thinking about the way she used to tease me. I'd jerked off to thoughts of her so many times in the shower that I thought I might rip my dick clean off.

Her mouth dropped open. "But you never said a thing. And you never looked anywhere, except my eyes," she shouted, pointing at her eyeballs with two fingers.

"Oh, yes, I did. You just never caught me." I let her know that everything she'd believed since we had been kids was basically a lie. "But your brother did."

Her mouth snapped shut. "Davey." She said his name like it tasted bad in her mouth. "What happened?"

"The night of your date, I couldn't keep my eyes off you, and I was so fucking jealous that I couldn't even speak clearly."

She let out a soft laugh. "I actually remember that." She shook her head. "You were talking gibberish before I left the house, right?"

"Yeah. Your brother called me out. Told me to stay the

hell away from you or I wasn't welcome in your home anymore."

"Seriously?"

I nodded. "Then, he made me promise that I'd never touch you. Ever. In my entire life."

Ivy threw her head back in disbelief and understanding. The two concepts crashed into her at the same time. I'd had years to reconcile this notion in my head, but she was just learning about it.

"And you agreed to that promise?" Her head cocked to the side, and I watched as her long blonde hair fell around her shoulders.

"I had to."

"Because you thought you'd lose everyone if you didn't."

She completely understood what her family had always meant to me. Ivy got me without my having to overexplain it.

"I did have my fingers crossed behind my back when I made it though, so maybe it doesn't count."

That made her laugh loudly. "Oh, that definitely voids it. Everyone knows that."

"I want you to know that I tried to think of ways to be with you and not piss off your brother, but he still brings up that damn promise, even now."

"What? Why?" She sounded ridiculously surprised. "We're grown adults. We can do whatever we want. Why does he even care so much about who I date? You'd think he'd want me to date someone like you."

"I think it's because he knows."

"Knows what?"

"That I've always wanted to be with you. But we made an agreement. And I feel like he's making me follow through on it for some reason."

"But that doesn't make any sense," she complained. "Also, can you please take off that costume? I'm over trying to have a serious conversation with Santa Claus."

I started immediately stripping out of the puffy jacket and oversize pants. The clothes I had on underneath were drenched in a layer of sweat. Being Santa was hard work.

"Ivy, I could use a shower." I pulled the white T-shirt from my body, showing her how wet it was, before I let it snap back to my chest with a slap.

"Okay."

Her eyes were looking everywhere but into mine, and I knew she still had questions. Hell, she probably had twelve years' worth of them.

"What is it?" I asked, and she looked at me with what looked like embarrassment in her eyes.

"I have clothes you can wear," she said.

Jealousy burned red hot through my veins. I tried to swallow, but my throat was dry.

"I'm not wearing some other dude's clothes," I snapped a little too harshly, but I was irrationally pissed. The thought of any other man touching her made me vicious.

"They're yours."

"What do you mean, they're mine?" I questioned.

She took a step back and folded her arms over her chest before explaining in rapid succession, "I have, like, four of your T-shirts and a pair of your gray sweats."

I couldn't help it, but I started laughing. "I wondered where those sweats had gone. They were my favorite."

She tried to hide a smile. "I know. But the thought of you walking around in gray sweatpants made me crazy."

I had no idea what the hell she was talking about. "Not

sure what that means."

An irritated sound slipped out of her mouth. "Look it up—gray sweats on guys. It's a thing."

"So, you stole my sweats," I said matter-of-factly.

"And I'd do it again." She wasn't even remotely sorry.

"What about the shirts?"

"They smelled like you. Or at least, they used to."

"Ivy." I practically growled her name. "I knew you liked me, but stealing my clothes borders on obsession."

"You call it obsessed; I call it creative acquisitioning."

I couldn't even act like I was the least bit upset at her thieving ways. She'd taken my clothes when I would have given them to her willingly.

"Take a shower with me."

Her eyes narrowed into a mischievous look that matched her expression. "I thought you wanted me in this stupid skirt."

"Now, I want you out of it."

"You promise it's not just sex?" She whispered the question, and for a second, I thought that she deserved something better than a shower for our first time. But I figured there would be so many more times after that it didn't matter.

"I promise it's not just sex. You could never be *just* anything. Now, get naked."

LONG LIVE SHOWER SEX

IVY

SAINT HAD JUST confessed so many things to me that I'd not only never known, but I had also never even suspected before today. I'd honestly believed that he never looked at me as anything other than a little sister. And I'd definitely had no idea that all those times I had been scantily clad, trying to tease him and make him want me, actually worked.

Saint was incredibly good at hiding his feelings from me. But now, I also understood exactly why—Davey. The person who was now at the top of my shit list. The more I thought about it, the angrier I got. Saint and I could have figured out this thing between us years ago and probably even been together this whole time. But, no, my brother had had to go and stick his nose where it didn't belong and try to control my dating life. Something he had no business doing.

"Ivy." Saint's voice interrupted my inner anger.

I tried to snap out of it. "Sorry. I was just getting mad at Davey in my head."

Saint started shaking his. "No. Leave him out of this for now. Tonight is about you and me and no one else. Plus, I told you to get naked."

"You did," I said, sounding agreeable.

"You're still in clothes," he said, pointing out the obvious, and I noticed that the hardness in his pants was back and on full display.

I widened my eyes as I stared at it, unable to look away. How did Saint walk with that thing between his legs?

"You're ... still ... in clothes," I stuttered as I pointed at it.

He dropped his joggers and pulled his shirt off in that sexy way that men did—by grabbing it from behind his head and tugging it over. "Now, I'm not."

I couldn't stop staring at *it*. There was no way that thing was going inside me without some serious effort. Or a hell of a lot of lubrication.

"If you make me ask you again, I'm going to spank you."

My mouth opened in shock. I'd never known Saint to talk this way, and I wasn't sure if I was turned on or a little scared. It might have been a combination of both. In order to avoid the spanking, not knowing if I'd enjoy it or not, I stepped out of my flimsy skirt and removed the top that I'd unbuttoned earlier. I was in nothing but a lace bra as Saint stepped toward me, his hardness poking me in the leg.

He reached around my back with both hands, and I felt the pressure release as he dropped my bra to the ground, setting my girls free. Before I could even move, he fell to his knees and started kissing me in places I hadn't been prepared for.

Tugging at his shoulders so he'd stop doing that and stand up, I called his name. "I need a shower too. I've been sweating all day, and, well, I don't want to smell like sweat."

Saint made me nervous. This was our first time being together, and the last thing I wanted was for my private parts to be a mixture of sweat and whatever else it naturally smelled like. It didn't seem like a stellar first impression if he threw his face down there.

Me, on the other hand? I couldn't have cared less what his giant dick smelled like. I was more concerned that I wouldn't be able to put it in my mouth, let alone anywhere else. Of course, a guy like Saint would be blessed in every area, making him even more damn alluring.

He reached for my hand, interlacing our fingers, and walked us toward the bathroom. I loved that he knew exactly where he was going even though he'd only been here a handful of times since I'd moved in. Usually, I would have been a little more self-conscious and aware of the lighting as I wandered around the halls, buck naked, but this was Saint we were talking about. I couldn't hide anything from him.

The water turned on, and I watched as he slipped his hand underneath the showerhead before adjusting the nozzle a little to the left for more heat. When he faced me, his fingertips skimmed down the side of my body, tracing my curves as his eyes stayed locked on my own. As a teenager, that had always made me frustrated, but tonight, it made me feel special.

"You are so damn beautiful," he said before adding, "it hurts."

I almost passed out with the weight of his compliment. No one had ever looked at me the way Saint currently was. And no man had ever said that kind of thing and meant it before. Drunk guys in bars excluded.

He removed his hand from my hip and tested the water one last time before stepping inside and reaching for me. The spray hit my hair, and I realized that I was going to have to wash it now that it was getting wet.

Saint grabbed my purple loofah and searched for which bottle was the soap before pouring a ridiculous amount onto it. I couldn't help the giggle that escaped from between my lips.

"You're laughing at me?" he asked, both dimples showing.

"That was so much soap." I pointed at it, and he simply shrugged.

"I don't have one of these things at my house. And I use bar soap. I don't know what the hell I'm doing," he admitted, and the charm seemed to ooze out of every pore.

"It's adorable," I said before giving him a kiss.

His lips were soaked from the water, and I liked the way it made them slippery. Snaking my tongue out of my mouth, I ran it along his bottom lip, and he groaned in response, his arm reaching out and pressing against the wall for balance.

"Wasn't expecting that," he breathed out, his eyes pressing shut before he reopened them.

The feel of the loofah surprised me at first, and I flinched before he started soaping me up. Saint moved slowly, his eyes following each and every move of his hands. A trail of suds went from my left breast to my hip, and his gaze was penetrating. I could *feel* him looking at me.

"Put your foot here," he directed, and I rested my heel on his thigh muscle.

Saint washed my feet and in between my toes before he lathered up his hands instead of the loofah and moved up my leg, toward my inner thigh.

My foot fell, and I was grateful that I didn't collapse altogether. "I need both feet on the floor," I said, and he grinned at that, clearly liking the effect he had on me.

His hand was between my legs, lathering up my most

sensitive area before moving to my ass and cleaning me there as well. When I tilted my head up to look at him, he was licking his lips, his dark, wet hair falling into his eyes. He stepped away from the spray of the water, letting it hit me, and I watched as the soap bubbles drifted away.

"I think you're clean now," he said before dropping to his knees without warning.

I'd stopped him earlier, afraid I might be sweaty down there, but now, I had no excuse.

His tongue lashed out, hitting my clit before taking all of me in one languid sweep. If I'd thought I might pass out before, it was nothing compared to how I was feeling now.

"Ivy," Saint growled against me, his breath hot as droplets of water continued to fall between us, "you taste so good."

My hand fisted his wet hair as he licked me again. And again.

"Like lavender?" I stupidly asked because that was the scent of my body wash.

"No," was all Saint said as he continued to ravish my lower body, making me quiver with each touch.

I had no idea how my legs weren't giving out from

under me, how I was still able to stand.

"Oh God, Saint," I stuttered as my orgasm started to build from somewhere deep inside me.

He licked me faster, his technique consistent, and that was all it took before I threw my head back, squeezed my eyes closed, and cried out with pleasure as my body jerked against his face.

He refused to stop. Even as I was coming down from my orgasm, his tongue continued to work in me. I had to physically push him away.

"That was amazing," I complimented, my breathing erratic.

He stood tall, his erection begging me for attention as it tapped me on the leg. One quick look at it, and I was intimidated yet again.

Before I could drop to my own knees in an attempt to get that thing in my mouth, Saint was holding my body against his, kissing all the thoughts from my head. I lost myself in the way his hands felt on my skin, wishing I could imprint this moment into my core memory file.

"My turn," I said, breaking the kiss and silently wishing myself luck.

I slowly lowered my body to the ground; my knees hitting the carpet with a soft thud. I was right. This penis had come from the gods. I looked at it and glanced up at Saint, who was peering down at me with curious eyes, before looking back at *it* again.

"Problem, love?" he asked with a wicked grin, and I felt determination rush through my veins.

"Nope," I said, popping the *P* before gripping the base of his dick with my hand and taking the tip of it inside my mouth.

A pleasure-filled groan ripped out of Saint, and I'd barely even done anything. That sound spurred me on even more. I took him as deep as I could without gagging and let my hand do the rest. The simultaneous movements seemed to work, and Saint slammed both palms against the sides of the shower—one on the tiles, the other on the glass wall. I was half-surprised he hadn't shattered it.

"Ivy. Jesus. It's so good." His breaths were labored, his voice ragged, and I was the one making him sound that way.

I moaned around the size of him, still working my hand at his base when I felt him grow even larger inside my mouth.

"I'm so close. Just like that. Don't stop, love."

Every time he called me *love*, teenage Ivy squealed from somewhere in the past. Saint started jerking and pulsing, and before I knew it, he had filled my mouth. I briefly considered spitting it all out, but I swallowed instead.

"You're a goddess," he said, and I actually felt like one.

FREAKING OUT

IVY

AFTER THE MOST intense shower I'd ever had in my life, we moved to the bedroom. I was grateful because my assumption about needing a little help to get him inside of me had been right. A shower would have never worked for that.

Saint was an attentive lover, paying attention to the way my body reacted to his touch and making me beg for more. I'd never felt so adored. When he pulled out of me for the third time, my body too sore for any more, I thought he might leave and go home. We'd crossed a line that couldn't be uncrossed, but I still didn't know what it meant.

"Do you have to go?" I wondered as I turned to face him, our naked bodies twisted in the sheets and each other.

"Go where?"

His arm reached for my hip, and he pulled me roughly against him, holding me there. Our bodies fit perfectly that way, like two pieces of the same puzzle. I could feel his heart beating against my back.

I must have fallen asleep because the next time I opened my eyes, we were still in the same position, but light was streaming through my curtains. It was morning. Saint's alarm started beeping from his phone, and his body jerked in response, his arm crushing me before his thumb traced lazy circles on my skin.

"Morning," he breathed out from behind me, his lips pressing against my shoulder.

I tried to turn my head to see him, but I couldn't move that far. "Morning."

He broke our contact, the cold air crashing around us as he quieted his alarm. "Shit," he mumbled under his breath.

I sat up and looked at him as my lower body ached. "What is it?"

"I have to go to the office. Davey's been texting."

"Okay," I said, trying to play it cool, but his sudden

change in demeanor had me worried.

"You're freaking out," he said, forcing me to admit that I was.

"A little."

"Let me handle Davey."

He tried to sound like he had it all under control, but I knew Saint better than that. He didn't. He was nervous and possibly second-guessing every single thing we'd done in the last twenty-four hours. His relationship with my brother was one of the most important things in his life, and I couldn't pretend like it wasn't.

That was when I realized that I hadn't thought any of this through. Not really. Not what it might all mean. I'd only known what I wanted, which was him. But what if getting it ruined everything else in the process? Or worse, what if in the light of day, Saint thought we'd made a mistake? I'd never be able to look him in the face again, and I'd lose one of my oldest and most trusted friends.

Saint pushed the sheets off of his body and stood up tall, his arms stretching over his body before he reached for the clothes from yesterday instead of the ones I'd stolen from him.

At least I'll get to keep those, I thought to myself.

What if that was all he left me with?

"You'll tell him about us?" I pushed because I was suddenly afraid to lose him and craved some kind of clarification into what we were now.

His blue eyes swept over the room before landing on mine. "I will." He nodded, and I felt myself relax only slightly.

"Today?" I continued to press him.

If what had happened between us was as life-changing as I considered it to be, there was no reason to wait. Everyone was going to find out soon enough.

"I'm not sure," he said, and my expression must have matched my disappointment because Saint was back on the bed, caressing my face. "Please understand, Ivy. I'll tell him. I just have to pick the right time."

"But Christmas is only three days away," I said as if he didn't know this information already.

Saint and his father always came to our house for Christmas dinner. It was going to be incredibly awkward now. Chalk that up to another thing I hadn't considered before diving headfirst into the shower with Saint.

I watched him swallow hard, his head shaking slightly.

"I know."

"I won't be able to pretend that I don't belong to you. Everyone at that table will know you've been inside me."

I was a piss-poor liar, and since I'd never been able to hide my feelings for Saint, I figured there was no way I'd be able to keep the fact that we'd finally done the deed from my family. They'd see it written all over my face.

A grin spread across his cheeks, those dimples making an appearance. He leaned closer to me and pressed a kiss to my mouth. When he tried to pull away, I grabbed the back of his head and kissed him again.

What if this was the last kiss he ever gave me?

"I'll tell your brother."

"Before Christmas dinner," I pushed, but he didn't agree. He ignored my statement altogether.

"Call you later, love."

And just like that, Saint walked out of my room and out of my apartment. I stayed in the bed until I heard his car start and drive off.

When I finally pulled myself together and walked into my kitchen, I noticed that he'd neatly folded our two costumes from last night. I knew that I needed to give them back to Cori, but a part of me wanted to put them in a memory box and hold on to them forever.

I'd never look at a Santa costume the same way again.

My phone started ringing out its tone for Cori, and I answered it before it went to voice mail, knowing that she'd start bombarding me with texts if I ignored her.

"Hey."

"What happened last night? Is he still there? Did you ruin the costumes? Please tell me you didn't ruin the costumes," she said in rapid-fire, and I blew out a breath once she finally stopped talking.

"I'll tell you at the salon. Well, as long as our moms aren't there. He just left. And the costumes are in tip-top shape. I'll bring them with me."

"My mom has today off. I think we're the only ones with appointments."

While most companies tended to slow down during the holidays, our hair salon only got busier. People flocked back into town each year like clockwork, and entire families of females made appointments months in advance to get their hair done for dinner and parties.

That space between Christmas and New Year's, when most other places heard crickets all day long? That was when we worked nonstop and made some of our best money of the year. Those who wanted to make an entrance when they walked into a room knew exactly where to come to make that happen. There was nothing like a fresh cut, color, extensions, or a stunning blowout, and Cori and I were two of the best in town.

Seeing my clients' faces for the first time after I spun their chair around to look in the mirror was something I'd never get tired of. I truly loved making women feel beautiful.

"Helloooo?" Cori shouted into the phone so loud that I had to pull it away from my ear.

"I'm here," I snapped because, now, my ear was ringing.

"Ugh. Just hurry up and get to the salon, so you can fill me in."

Cori knew that I'd never talk about Saint once a client was sitting in the chair. Hearing all about their personal business was one thing, but contributing with stories about mine was a line I didn't dare cross. Not that most seemed to mind or even notice.

People loved talking about themselves. I actually enjoyed it, to be honest. There wasn't a single day that I didn't learn something new.

I wonder what I'll learn today, I thought to myself as I packed up my purse, grabbed the costumes, and bundled up in an oversize jacket.

When I got to my car, it was covered in snow, but the windshield and all of the windows had been scraped clean of the ice I knew had covered it.

Saint.

If that man didn't tell my brother about us, I was going to blurt it out in the middle of Christmas dinner and blow the whole thing up. There was zero chance I'd be able to spend all evening with him and not cave.

PROMISE BREAKER

SAINT

'D BEEN GIVING myself a pep talk the entire drive over to the office from Ivy's house. Twenty minutes of nonstop psychobabble, where I oscillated between being the worst friend on the face of the earth, who had performed the most inexcusable act, to trying to convince myself that I hadn't done anything wrong and that Ivy and I were two consenting adults who deserved to be happy.

Even if it is with my best friend's little sister.

Oh God, I was definitely the worst, and Davey was never going to forgive me.

When I walked into the office kitchen for some coffee, Davey was already there along with a couple of employees.

"Morning, brother," he said, his long blond hair pulled

into a man bun that I swore only he could pull off. "You look like hell," he said easily before narrowing his eyes. "What'd you do last night?"

"Nothing." I tried to sound nonchalant, but he knew me better than almost anyone, so lying was hard.

"Didn't you have that volunteer thing with Ivy?"

Acting like I'd forgotten all about it already even though it was seared into my brain like fire from a hot poker, I gave him a nod. "Oh yeah. Lots of kids. So many kids." I concentrated on pouring some creamer into my coffee and stirred it with a tiny straw.

"You were Santa, right? Have any pictures?" He was teasing me now, and that little change in his voice calmed me down.

If Davey knew what had happened last night, the last thing he'd be doing was joking around.

I racked my brain for a second before answering. "I actually don't have any pictures. All the kids do though. There was a photographer there."

"What was Ivy doing? How is she? I feel like I haven't seen her in months."

Your sister is a fucking angel who tastes like sin, and

I'll never get enough of her pussy in my mouth.

"She was an elf," I said.

The hottest elf I've ever laid eyes on. You should have seen her ass in that skirt. Hell, you should have seen her ass out of that skirt.

"What?" Davey's voice broke through my thoughts, and for a second, I thought I might have said all of that out loud. Pretty sure I wouldn't be standing upright if I had though. "She was an elf? HA! Please tell me you at least have a picture of that."

"Nah. Cori might," I suggested like I couldn't be less interested, and he looked momentarily satisfied.

"I knew I should have swung by to see that shit in person." He slapped a palm on my shoulder before letting me know that we had a call with our lawyer, Larry.

We were trying to wrap up this lawsuit before the end of the year. A guy out in California was trying to claim that we'd stolen his app idea, but there was nothing original about creating a dating app for successful individuals. Not to mention the fact that ours was locally based.

Unlike other apps, you couldn't update your location

and try to meet someone while you were traveling. Basically, if you left the state, the app didn't work. That was the whole point though—to meet someone where you were based, where you wanted to live, or where you planned on settling down.

There had been a handful of naysayers at first, claiming that no one would want something so "small-minded," they called it. But fortunately for me and Davey, they had been wrong, and our instincts had been right. We had one of the most successful online businesses in the state.

"Larry says this dude doesn't stand a shot. He's just trying to flex his muscles, so to speak," Davey said as he made a face.

"He has no case," I said, hoping my tone reflected my irritation.

This entire thing was a waste of time, resources, and money. There was zero chance this arrogant douchebag from California was going to win, but in order for us to not lose, we had to provide documentation of origination, app filings, and all sorts of other things. It was a colossal pain in the ass.

"I know. I wonder all the time what his angle even is," Davey said as we walked toward our offices. They were across the hall from each other, so we stopped in the middle and continued our conversation. "Like, what's the point of doing this to us? We're not his competition. He's in Los Angeles, for fuck's sake. There're a million rich people there."

I had wondered about this guy so often that it kept me up at night. Had we wronged this dude at some point in our life? After researching him and his company for hours on end, I'd realized that we'd never met him and had zero mutual friends. This wasn't some kind of personal vendetta against us; the guy just had too much time on his hands.

"From what I've gathered, he's bored. And he's the kind of guy who thinks everyone is out to steal from him. His parents are loaded. He's never had to work a day in his life. He has an entire staff that searches the Apple and Android stores for anything even remotely similar to any of his creations, and then he does this."

"He sues them?"

"Yeah." I nodded my head. I'd only just found that

part out yesterday morning, so I hadn't told him yet. "The worst part is, he stops most people before they even get off the ground."

"That's horrible." Davey grimaced.

"It's definitely not good."

Our core belief was to support our fellow content creators. We often spoke at conferences about how to start your own businesses and create your own sellable app. Davey and I believed that one way we could give back to others was through sharing information. Not proprietary information, mind you, just knowledge. Between the two of us, we had a wealth of it with nowhere for it to go.

"Guys like that deserve to get their asses kicked."

I gave him a nod, letting him know that I basically agreed, while I silently prepared for the fact that once I told him about me and Ivy, it would be my ass he was attempting to kick. "Let me grab a file from my office, and we'll take the call in yours."

"Sounds good," he said before walking away while I tried to work up the damn nerve to let him know that I liked his sister as more than a friend.

THE CALL WITH Larry took less than twenty minutes. He'd said the claim should be wrapped up before Christmas, but we'd been dealing with this on and off for months already, so Davey and I weren't convinced. I wanted to be hopeful that the suit would be dropped once and for all, but I wasn't.

"All right, well, now, what do we do?" Davey asked after ending the call, and I shrugged.

"We wait."

"I didn't mean with the lawsuit, bro. I meant with our day." He sounded so excited, and I hated how fucking conflicted I felt inside.

I needed to get it all out in the open once and for all. It wasn't like Ivy and I'd been hiding a relationship from him for months or anything.

Being with Ivy was a no-brainer, especially after last night. There was zero chance I'd be walking away from her without a fight, so why was telling her brother so damn difficult? I was a grown-ass man, but whenever I thought about coming clean, I reverted into that seventeen-year-old kid who had tried like hell to stand by his word—even if his fingers were crossed behind his back.

That stupid fucking promise rang in my ears. Davey had been dead serious when he asked me to make it, and in one night, I'd blown the entire thing to bits. There was a high probability that he'd never forgive me, and I had no idea how we'd continue working together if that happened.

Could I lose half my family and still live happily with the other?

That was my dilemma.

"What's eating you? You have that look on your face," Davey said, bringing me back to the present.

"What look?" I asked, wondering what he'd say.

"The look where you're keeping something from me," he pushed, and I swallowed around the lump in my throat.

"No, I don't."

"What'd you say you did last night?"

That was twice now that he'd asked that particular question.

"I told you already. Nothing."

He pushed back from his chair and stood up, and I instinctively did the same. Davey definitely knew more than he'd let on earlier.

"The kind of nothing that involves your car being parked at my sister's house all night?"

I gasped, almost choking on the intake of air. I felt like I was suffocating.?"

"The least you could do is be a fucking man and admit it to my face," he growled, and we both stood tall, our shoulders back, our chests puffed out.

"I was going to tell you," I tried to say, but he put a hand up.

He didn't want to hear my bullshit excuses, and I wasn't sure I blamed him, but it was all out in the open now.

There was no going back from here. And honestly, I'd needed it there because I felt more in control than I had thirty seconds ago.

"You promised."

"I was seventeen!" I shouted back because I was starting to get pissed off. This was fucking stupid.

"You. Made. Me. A. Promise." He enunciated each word as I watched his hand ball into a fist.

I braced myself for the punch he was about to deliver. I'd give him just this one before I started hitting back.

MONSTER PANTS

IVY

I WALKED INTO the salon an hour before my first client was set to arrive. There were things to prep and get ready for, but mostly, it was so that I could fill Cori in on my evening with Saint without any prying ears.

"Here are the costumes," I shouted into the void.

I wasn't sure if she'd run them out to her car or not, so I didn't put them at her station, instead tossing them on top of the check-in counter. I dropped my purse into one of the drawers at my station and pocketed my phone. Hair stations were cramped enough already without adding anything extra to the space. Santa's coat alone was a giant mass of material that stood about two feet tall, even when folded.

Cori wandered around the corner from the supply

closet in the back, a knowing grin on her face before she literally started squealing like we were back in the old high-school hallways. She ran up to me and gave me a hug.

"Do you feel different?" she asked, her brown eyes inquisitive.

"It's not like the guy took my virginity." Although he had done things that I'd never had done to me before.

"I can't believe this finally happened. We've been pining over him for years."

I definitely noticed the way she'd said *we*, and it made me smile.

"I need to know every dirty detail." She suggestively wagged her eyebrows at me. "And I do mean, every single one. The dirtier, the better."

The second she said those words, my mind flashed back to the shower. And the bedroom. And each delectable moment in between.

"You're ridiculous, but I love it." I tried to play it all off, but I was a ball of conflicting emotions inside. "Did you turn on the computer and set up the credit card machine?" I asked even though I knew she hadn't.

"No," she said.

Cori never touched the electronic equipment, claiming that she was cursed when it came to everything, except her phone. I made my way back to the machine and flipped it into the on position, and I waited for it to slowly come to life. We really needed to update some of our machines.

"You're stalling. Why are you stalling?" She leaned her elbows on the counter and waited for me to start talking.

"I don't know." I stood up tall and faced her, not knowing where to start.

Last night had been incredible, but this morning had kind of sucked. And now, Saint was at the office with my brother, and I still hadn't heard a single word from him. Trust me, I kept checking my phone like it might have turned itself off or something.

"Was it bad?" The way her mouth twisted into a scowl had me rolling my eyes. "Oh, dear God, was he bad in bed?"

"No," I said with a slight laugh. "He was definitely not bad in bed."

"Thank you." She looked up toward the ceiling like

she was having a conversation with God himself. "How big was his wanker?"

She held her hands in front of her face and moved them closer and farther apart before stopping on what would be considered small by any standards. I actually thought about not telling her, but she was my best friend, and I needed to tell someone about it.

My eyes grew wide in order to emphasize what I was about to say. "It was unreal. Saint has a monster living between his legs."

Her face twisted into disbelief, like I had to be exaggerating. "You've been in love with him your whole life. Of course you're going to think it's big."

I started shaking my head vigorously. "I'm not ... it's huge. I don't understand how he just walks around all day with that thing. It has to get in the way."

"So, you're telling me that he's got the biggest D you've ever seen *and* he's great in the sack?"

"Basically, yeah," I said, realizing that both of those things were true and I was so done for.

"And his kissing skills? Tell me he doesn't slobber or force-feed you his tongue." She stuck her tongue out and moved it around like a crazy person trying to lick the air.

"He's a grown man. He knows how to kiss," I said with a laugh. "I think the slobber and tongue-stabbing only happened when we were younger."

She made a sick sound of gagging mixed with her breath getting stuck in her throat. "You would think that"—she pointed at me with one finger—"but you'd be wrong. It can happen at any age."

"Learn something new every day."

"Gotta admit, Ivy, I was going to be pretty disappointed if all of this had been for nothing."

"It still might have been," I breathed out my internal thought before I could stop it from coming out of my mouth.

She put her hands on her hips and cocked her head to the side, taking her violet hair with her. I watched as it all moved in the same direction in one fluid motion, like a work of art. "What do you mean? Ivy, what happened?"

I started shaking my head. "Last night was amazing. I mean, I couldn't have dreamed up anything better. But this morning, he was weird."

"Weird how? Like he regretted it? Like you shouldn't

have done it?" she asked, her face determined and her lips scowling. "A little late for that, buddy. I'll kill him."

I reached out and touched her shoulder. "I don't think he regretted it—"

"But …" she interrupted, like she always did.

"But he did mention Davey and some promise that he'd made to my brother when they were seventeen. He seemed worried about that."

"Seventeen!" she shouted into the otherwise empty salon, and I stopped myself from covering my ears. "That was a hundred years ago. Who cares anymore? And promise? What promise?"

"My brother made Saint promise he'd never touch me. Ever. Not even as adults." When I said the words out loud, to someone other than myself, I realized how ridiculous they sounded.

"First of all,"—Cori held up a single finger—"that's stupid. Second"—another finger—"everything makes so much more sense now."

"Explain," I demanded with just one word.

"I always knew that Saint was into you, but I never understood why he didn't make a move. Why he tried so hard to pretend like he wasn't. And now, I get it."

"The promise," I said as I tried to accept it.

"Davey would have killed him back then," she said matter-of-factly. "And I get it. Big brothers are crazy people when it comes to their little sisters. They're irrational and insane."

"You can say that again."

The sounds of a car beeping and doors slamming shut diverted my attention outside. Both of our clients had arrived at the same time … albeit early. I hadn't even prepped yet, but that was my own fault, not theirs.

"Hey"—Cori reached into her pocket and pulled out the keys to the front door—"Saint's a big boy. And if last night was even half as great as you're making it out to be, he won't be able to stay away from you for long. And he'll lose Davey in the process if he has to."

She sounded so damn sure of her assessment of my situation. I was far more uncertain as I pulled my phone from my back pocket and checked it again. Still nothing. No texts, no missed calls, and no messages waiting in my DMs.

"And don't do that," she added, pointing at my phone

as she walked toward the door to let our guests inside.

"Do what?"

"Give him all the power," she explained, and I put the phone back down. "By waiting for him to text you or call you, it mentally puts you in a position of weakness. You're allowed to text him first. And you don't need permission to do it. All waiting is going to do is make you feel bad. And make you obsess."

The door swung open, and our two clients waltzed inside, shaking the freshly fallen snow off of their jackets as we all said, "Hello," and, "Good morning," at the same time.

Cori wandered back in my direction before whispering one final nugget of advice. "I know it sucks, waiting for the guy to reach out when all you want to do is talk to him and make sure you're on the same page. Or at least heading in the same direction. We let them make the first move because we don't want to come off as needy or clingy. But, Ivy, if a guy can't handle a little communication after a night of insanely hot sex, then he doesn't deserve you."

"Amen to that!" one of the women shouted.

I was mortified that she'd overheard, but I knew better than to engage. Thankfully, it was Cori's client and not mine, so I wouldn't be subjected to her fifty questions during our session. My client was too busy, texting on her phone, to eavesdrop or even know what we were talking about.

Must be nice, I thought to myself as bitterness tore through me. I was competing with my client, who was most likely sending a text to her kid or a friend, for Pete's sake!

If I was already behaving this irrationally after only a couple of hours, I was never going to survive. So, I grabbed my phone and sent Saint a text before I could talk myself out of it. Cori was right; I needed to take initiative and at least attempt some semblance of self-control.

DID DAVEY KILL YOU, OR ARE YOU STILL ALIVE?

I held my breath and waited. He read it almost instantly, but there were no dancing dots or any indication that he planned on responding.

And when almost three hours passed with not even a single word from him on any platform, I started thinking that he might be avoiding me.

He was definitely ignoring me. It took two seconds to respond to a text message, and I'd learned that when a man wanted you, you knew how he felt.

What the hell did it mean if Saint stopped talking to me?

LOSING MY BEST FRIEND

SAINT

I STOOD THERE, bracing myself for the hit I'd convinced myself I deserved, but it never came. Like I'd said, I was going to give Davey the first punch before I started swinging back.

"Do it already," I shouted, definitely creating a scene for those who were, unfortunately, still in the office.

"You want me to hit you?" he questioned loudly, his eyes blazing fire.

"You get one," I growled in response, letting him know that this wasn't a game I'd be lying down and rolling over for.

"Will it stop you from hooking up with my sister?"

A twisted laugh tore from deep in my throat. "No."

"You sure about that?" he pushed, most likely working

up the anger to deliver one hell of a hit.

"Positive."

"You asked for it." Davey took a single step in my direction, and I flexed my right hand in preparation before he bent over in half and started cracking up.

My heartbeat was erratic, and I swore I could feel the blood pulsing through my veins just under the skin. I blinked a few times quickly to make sure I wasn't seeing things, but Davey looked like he might keel over and die from laughing so hard.

"I'm confused," I said the words slowly, methodically. Maybe this was some sort of trick or trap. If I lowered my defenses, I'd be an easier target.

Davey looked up at me, his body still bent over as it shook wildly. "You should have seen your face," he tried to say, but it came out in broken syllables that I managed to understand.

"What the hell is going on?" I pushed back on the heels of my feet and reached for a chair to brace my weight on.

When he finally stopped his laughing fit, he stood upright and blew out some over-the-top breaths, followed by high-pitched *wooo* sounds.

"Are you finished?" I asked, still not quite believing that this wasn't some sort of prank that might backfire on me at any moment.

"Oh man," Davey breathed out. "Your face. Shit. You were really going to hit me, weren't you?"

"I still might," I said, and he started laughing again.

If he didn't stop, we'd be here all day like this.

He put both hands in the air. "Okay, okay. I'm done … I think."

Right when he'd finally calmed himself down, his fiancée, Samantha, waltzed into the office, her brown hair in a bun that matched the kind Davey sported. How had I never noticed that before? They had matching fucking hairstyles. I wondered if Ivy had done it just to mess with them, and I stopped myself from grabbing my phone and sending her a text to ask.

"Did I miss it? Darn, I missed it, didn't I?" Samantha asked as she sat down in one of the seats in Davey's office, clearly out of breath, and I shot her a look, to which she answered, "What? I ran here. I hate running."

I continued to glare at her with a confused expression.

"Why did you run here?" I asked, wondering what she knew that I obviously didn't that was so important that she'd chosen to run here in order to not miss it.

Davey walked over to his fiancée and bent down to give her a sweet kiss on the mouth before heading toward his own chair and sitting down in it. "Babe, you only missed the part where he thought I was going to hit him and he was gearing up to hit me back," he said with a slight giggle.

"I still don't understand why that's so funny," I complained as my phone vibrated in my pocket. I pulled it out, saw a text from Ivy, read it, and considered responding, but I put it away just as quickly. I'd fill her in on everything later.

"Because, idiot, I'm not going to hit you for liking my sister," he explained, like that was common knowledge and anyone with half a brain could have figured that part out.

"You're joking, right?"

"Why would I be joking?" Davey sounded so convinced of his sanity, like I was the crazy one for even thinking he'd be mad at me. I felt like I was in some kind of alternate universe, where everything was backward and nothing made sense.

"Because you bring up that stupid promise I made all the time!" I threw my hand in the air and started pacing.

"I only did that because I was trying to get you to finally come clean. I figured if I kept bringing it up, you'd eventually tell me to fuck off."

I stopped moving. "What are you talking about?"

Samantha cleared her throat, forcing our attention toward her. "We know you like her, Saint."

"Of course I like her," I said as I exhaled.

"You made that painfully obvious when you tried to sabotage our business before it even got off the ground," Davey said with a cocky smirk, and I felt my shoulders tense.

I hadn't meant to cause us any problems, but I had done exactly that.

Ivy had started dating this guy, Ian, and for whatever reason, I thought she might be getting serious with him. The kind of serious that might include a ring and children at some point. My brain short-circuited whenever I even thought about her with someone who wasn't me.

So, I created a fake profile for Ian on our app even though he wasn't financially qualified to be on it, and I made sure he matched with at least twenty women. I had known his phone number, so I signed him up for text messages since the app wasn't on his phone, but the second the messages started being delivered, it had taken him less than ten minutes to download our app and start chatting with his matches.

"That was one time. And I knew we could say there was a glitch in the system," I argued in response, but I knew I'd fucked up.

"Funny how the glitch only happened to my sister's boyfriend," Davey said before spinning in his chair like a child.

"You always knew it was me?" I asked because he'd never come out and said it before now. And up until this moment, I'd always denied having anything to do with it. Even the engineers on our team had claimed they weren't sure how it happened.

"Everyone knew it was you," Samantha said before adding, "except the one person who should have."

I tilted my head to the side and snapped my lips closed.

"Ivy. She never even suspected you, you know that? She thought it was Davey the whole time. She was convinced that he was trying to sabotage her relationship."

"And I let her believe it," Davey said with a nod.

"Why would you do that?" I finally pulled one of the other chairs out and sat in it.

"Because you obviously weren't ready."

"Ready for what?" I asked out loud, feeling like sort of stupid.

"To admit that you had feelings for her. To do what it took to be with her," Samantha answered instead of Davey.

I realized that the two of them must have had multiple conversations about this subject before. She shot Davey a look, and he interpreted it the way that couples seemed to be able to do after being together for a while. They spoke without words.

"You were going to let Davey hit you?" Samantha asked me, her eyebrows lifting.

I nodded but clarified my intentions. "Once. I was going to let him hit me one time."

"And then what were you going to do?" She was

grinning, and I got the distinct impression that she was enjoying this.

"I was going to start hitting back."

"Why?"

"Why what?"

"Why were you going to hit Davey—your best friend, your brother—back?"

Sitting down for this discussion was making me anxious, so I shoved out of the chair, stood up, and started pacing the room again.

"Because the first punch would have been a courtesy. I'd broken the promise I'd made to him. He deserved to hit me for it." As I said the words out loud, they made perfect sense to me. They were logical, and the look on Davey's face told me that he agreed.

"But after that courtesy hit, then what?"

If she was trying to bait me, I wasn't sure why or to what end. Was Davey pissed at me or not? It sure didn't seem like he was.

Samantha kept talking. "It stopped being about you breaking a promise to Davey and became about what instead?"

"It was always about Ivy. Is that what you're trying to get at?" I was growing agitated, and her word games were making my head hurt.

"But what about her?"

"I'm in love with her, okay? Is that what you fucking want to hear?" I looked away from Samantha and focused on Davey as I confessed the next part. "I'm in love with your sister, and I have been since I was seventeen. Probably even before then."

Samantha clapped her hands together like she'd won the grand prize on a game show.

Davey let out a, "Ha! I knew it! The night she went on that date with Jordan Ramsey, I thought you might rip his head clean off before they walked out the door."

"I thought about it," I said, feeling just as irrational now as I had back then. "That's when you made me promise to never touch your sister. *Ever.*" I emphasized the last word, and he gave me a knowing nod.

"I know. I meant it then. It's just something you don't do. We were brothers, and I couldn't have you fucking it all up by messing around with my sister. She'd been obsessed with you since we were ten."

"So, you don't mean it anymore?" I absolutely needed Davey to spell it all out for me. It wasn't going to stop me from being with Ivy, but his approval would make my life a hell of a lot more enjoyable.

"Nah," he said like the idea of me and Ivy didn't even faze him in the slightest. "But don't even think about telling me anything gross. If you mention the things you do with my sister, even in passing, I will hit you."

It was my turn to laugh. Finally. I would never peep a word about his goddess of a sister or all the filthy things I planned on doing to her body. "Agreed. Your parents will be okay with it, right?"

I wasn't honestly worried about Mr. and Mrs. Simpson, but it still felt right to at least ask.

"My parents will probably throw the two of you a fucking party. This is their dream union. I think they've loved you as long as Ivy has."

They'd certainly always made me feel that way.

"I'd better go talk to them."

I wanted their verbal blessing as well. And since Christmas was only a few days away, it seemed like the right thing to do was give them a heads-up instead of ambushing them during dinner.

Davey grabbed his keys from the top desk drawer and pushed to a stand. "We're coming for that."

I knew there was no use in trying to talk them out of witnessing what I was about to do, so I didn't even try. As the three of us walked out of the office and into the parking garage, I blew out a breath of relief, the white air swirling around my mouth.

Today could have gone in a completely different direction. I'd seen it all play out in my head a hundred times, and it had never once ended this way. I still had my best friend, and I was about to get the girl of my dreams too.

Merry freaking Christmas to me.

MY CHRISTMAS WISH

IVY

"**S**TILL NOTHING?" CORI asked as we started our closing procedures at the salon.

I switched off the computer and printed the credit card statement for the day before walking to the back room to wash out some trays and make sure all the caps were where they belonged and closed tight.

"Nope," I said, trying not to convey any emotion at all even though I was feeling a million things. None of them good.

"It doesn't make sense. Saint can't just ghost you, you know? He's not some guy you met at a bar or at the grocery store. There's too much history there."

I knew she was only trying to make me feel better, but until I actually heard from Saint, nothing was going to cheer me up.

"Maybe he got what he wanted. What if I was just a challenge and he didn't realize it until it was too late?" I asked because the awful thought had crossed my mind.

Some guys lived for the girls they couldn't have, but others didn't always know when the resistance was the one thing propelling them forward. I could imagine that if Saint felt that way, he'd be struggling with how to tell me. He wouldn't want to hurt me, but he also couldn't lie about it. He'd be so torn.

"I don't think that's it, Ivy. Truly. I'd be surprised."

"I want to believe you," I admitted before she interrupted my thoughts.

"But you don't."

My head swung in her direction. "I'm not sure what to think, to be honest."

We finished cleaning up, and I got a head start on prepping for my early morning client. The more time I had to sleep in, the better. I set up my station with everything I needed and pulled my purse out of the drawer I kept it in.

"You work tomorrow?" I wasn't sure of her schedule since we all kept different hours and handled our calendar on our own.

"Nine until four. Do you want to grab a drink or anything?" Even though she knew I wasn't in the mood, she still gave me the option to avoid going home, if that was what I needed.

"I'd be shit company."

"You're always shit company," she teased, and it made me laugh. It felt like the first time I'd done that all day.

"No. I'm pretty tired."

"Especially after all your extracurriculars with Monster Cock last night."

She wasn't wrong. Saint had kept me up way past my bedtime. And even though my heart was hurting for it today, I'd still never take last night back.

"Please don't call him that." I winced and grabbed between my thighs. I was still sore, and each time I went to the bathroom, I was reminded of that fact.

"I won't. At least, not to his face."

The two of us walked out of the salon and into the frigid night air. I locked the door behind us, and we made sure we each got into our cars safely before pulling onto the main road together. It was something we did so that neither of us was ever alone when we left. We also checked the backseats for murderers before we drove off. If you weren't a female, you probably wouldn't understand.

ONCE I WAS back in my apartment, the memories hit me with the force of a flash flood. Saint's mouth on mine. His tongue inside me. His hands squeezing, grasping, and tugging at me. Shaking my head to make them go away, I walked into my bedroom, opened the nightstand drawer, and pulled out a folded piece of paper.

Every year since I had been eight years old, I'd made a separate, private Christmas list for Santa. It wasn't like the one I had given to my parents, asking for a horse and Hot Wheels or gift cards. That list had hung on the fridge next to Davey's and eventually Saint's until Christmas morning.

This other list only had one thing on it. And each year, it was exactly the same.

1.) Please let Saint LaCroix love me back.

That was it.

I still had the one I had written in tenth grade. Kept it under my pillow each night during the month of December. It had become a personal tradition of sorts. I'd read somewhere that putting wishes under your head at night while you slept helped them come true. I figured that I'd take all the help I could get when it came to Saint, so I did it. For twenty-five nights, every December, for years.

Last night, when Saint had been here, I'd grabbed the old note before he could find it and stuffed it into my nightstand drawer. I would have been mortified if he had seen it. It was one thing for him to know that I had a crush on him, but for him to see it written down on a note that I slept with at night? That seemed a little more than just embarrassing.

I thought about sending Saint another text, but one ignored message had proven to be more than enough for me to handle. I was currently sitting on my bed, holding the note in my hand, half-tempted to tear it in half and never look at it again. If he didn't love me by now, he was never going to. At some point, I needed to accept my reality and move on.

A hard knock at my front door made me jump, and I quickly shoved the still-intact note underneath my pillow.

"Ivy?" Saint's voice reverberated as he let himself inside.

I didn't lock my front door?

"What are you doing here?" I asked tentatively as I rounded the corner of my room to find him standing in the entryway.

I wasn't sure what this meant—him showing up, unannounced, after I hadn't heard a peep from him. My heart raced and leaped, and my mind started spinning scenarios I wished so hard were true.

"I'm so sorry," he said before taking me in his arms and squeezing.

He was apologizing. For last night. He regretted it—or something equally as horrifying. My arms fell from their position around his back, landing at my sides, as I stopped hugging him.

The second I did that, he reached for my chin and tilted it upward, toward his mouth. "You have it wrong, love. I'm sorry that I didn't text you back. I was taking care of some housekeeping," he said with a wink before his lips were on mine, kissing me like he couldn't wait another second to do it.

I wanted to kiss him back, to lose all of my resolve and give in, but I stopped myself. Breaking the kiss, I shook my head and stepped back to give my body space from his.

"Care to explain what you're talking about?" My tone came out harsher than I'd meant, but I wasn't sorry about it.

His statement about housekeeping had me confused. What did that even mean?

He reached for my hand—a simple gesture that I wanted to resist, but I allowed it. His fingers moved across my skin, but I wasn't even holding on to him the way he was to me. It was a silent answer to an unasked question.

"I talked to Davey," he finally said.

I ripped my hand from his without warning. I hadn't meant to do it, but it was a knee-jerk response to his statement.

"Is that where you've been all day? What happened?"

"Let's sit. Can we sit?"

He didn't wait for me to answer before he started walking in the direction of my living room. I followed because of course I did.

We both sat on my favorite couch, not on either end of it, but so close that our knees pressed together as our bodies faced each other. He filled me in on what had happened at the office with Davey and eventually Samantha too. To say I was shocked would be an understatement. Not because Davey wasn't angry with him, but because all of these people seemed to be involved and invested in the state of my and Saint's relationship.

"Samantha knew I liked you. I mean, I'd told her so a bunch of times before. Even when I had other boyfriends," I admitted, and it made him smile even though it made me feel like a bit of a schmuck.

I shouldn't have been dating anyone while I had feelings for someone else. Then again, I couldn't imagine ever *not* having feelings for Saint, so by that logic, I'd never have dated anyone, and I'd have become an old spinster lady with fifteen cats.

"Speaking of other boyfriends," he said slowly and with a slight wince.

"What about them?" I had no idea what he was trying to hint at.

"Remember Ian?"

"The douchebag who was on your app and left me for some rich, old lady he had been messaging for weeks? Yeah, I remember," I said with a frown.

Even though Ian had vehemently denied setting up the initial profile, he still met some of the women he'd matched with behind my back, eventually breaking up with me for one of them, who had claimed she didn't care that he wasn't wealthy enough to be on it in the first place. She'd wanted a man's undivided attention, and he had been more than willing to give it to her.

"I'm the one who made his profile."

"What?" I asked with a half-laugh. "That was you? I always thought it was Davey."

"I know. He told me that today." Saint placed his hand on top of my thigh and squeezed before keeping it there. I liked the way it felt.

"Why did you do it?" I asked, wondering how I'd never put those particular pieces together, but then again, I never thought Saint liked me as more than a friend, so I never even thought it was his doing.

"Because he was lasting too long. You weren't going

to break up with him."

I laughed hard then before calming down. "Yes, I would have. I mean, eventually. I always did."

"No one had ever stuck around that long before. I needed to make him go away before he proposed or something."

Placing my hand on top of his, I interlaced our fingers and tried to hide my smile. I felt so satisfied to know that he was just as crazy about me as I was about him. "You know, some might classify that behavior as obsessive or unhealthy, Saint."

"I call it creative interference," he said with a grin, mimicking my response from last night.

I leaned toward him, and our lips pressed together. If it were anyone else in the world, I would have thought they were batshit crazy and steered clear of them. But this was Saint LaCroix we were talking about, the guy who had loved me almost as long as I'd loved him, but unlike me, he'd had to hide his feelings and pretend like he didn't have them. I couldn't blame him for getting creative.

"One more thing," he said, putting up a finger, and I gave him a look that told him to keep going. "I talked to your parents earlier. That's what took me so long to get over here."

Of all the things that Saint could have told me, I hadn't even thought about that. My parents loved him, so I couldn't imagine them having any issue whatsoever with us being a couple. But what if I was wrong?

"What'd they say?" I was suddenly curious as to their reaction or response.

A giant smile lit up his whole face, and both dimples appeared on his cheeks. "That it was about damn time and that I'd better not fuck it up or I'd be sorry."

That sounded about right ... *on both fronts.*

And I had to admit that I agreed with them even though I wasn't even remotely worried. There was zero chance that either Saint or I would mess this up after taking so long to get to this place. I thought that when you finally figured out where you belonged and with who, you fought like hell to keep it.

Then, I remembered the fact that he'd ignored me all day long and not responded to my text, and for some reason, setting those boundaries felt important in this moment. "You could have texted me back, you know?

That was a bit of a dick move."

He blew out a breath. "I got your text right in the middle of my conversation with Davey, and I meant to respond after, but we all went over to your parents' house."

"Why did Davey and Sam go with you?"

He shook his head and laughed. "They insisted. Said they wouldn't miss that conversation for the world. Your parents practically broke out the champagne. Samantha said she would have been offended if she wasn't so damn happy for us."

I started imagining the three of them storming into Mom and Dad's home, demanding to see them and telling them the news. I shook my head and focused on my original point. "Still, you could have sent me a message. You left me hanging all day, and my mind went through a million scenarios. None of them good, Saint. You can't do that to me."

"I know." He wrapped his arm around my lower back. "I'm sorry. It won't happen again."

"It takes two seconds to write me back," I complained, still forcing the issue because not hearing from him had ruined my whole day.

"You're right. Let me make it up to you," he said before moving off the couch and dropping to his knees.

This man always seemed to be on them for me.

And I wouldn't have it any other way.

If he wants to worship at my altar, who am I to stop him? I thought to myself as I threw my head back and moaned.

It was going to be a long night, and I was going to relish in every single second of it, knowing full well that it would happen again because this man was finally mine. I thought about the private Christmas list hiding underneath my pillow and smiled to myself. I couldn't wait to tell Saint about it.

After he finished apologizing, of course.

EPILOGUE
CHRISTMAS DINNER

IVY

ONE YEAR LATER

THE SEVEN OF us, including Saint's dad, sat around my parents' dining room table, which was set to perfection for Christmas dinner with holiday-themed place settings, like we did each and every year at this time. It used to just be the six of us. Samantha was the newest addition, but even she'd been making an appearance for two years now. Her and my brother had gotten married three months ago, and I was so excited to have a sister! She had three of her own, but they all lived out of town, and none of them were as fabulous as me. Her words, not mine.

I thought she just liked my hair skills. I came in handy.

I hoped that one day, we'd be able to make this family dinner an even eight adults, but that would mean that Saint's dad would have to find an actual girlfriend who stuck around for longer than two months. We had little hope for that though, no matter how hard we pushed. Saint had even threatened to put him on the app, and he'd threatened to disown him if he did.

Speaking of the app, there had been a lawsuit with some super rich guy that seemed to drag on forever. Apparently, the man was relentless when it came to companies developing things that he deemed too similar to his own. After months of working every angle he could possibly think of, the case was finally dismissed. He had nothing on Saint and my brother and was forced to walk away empty handed. None of us realized just how much it weighed on our subconscious until it was finally over with. The relief was palpable.

Sam kept placing her hand on her nonexistent belly, but every time she touched it, we all oohed and aahed like she was a magical being who was doing something no one had ever done before.

"Stop," she whined, shaking her head and moving her

hand away.

"We're just excited," my dad said with a grin.

Even though he had claimed that all he wanted was a healthy grandchild, we all knew he secretly hoped it would be a little boy. He couldn't help it.

"And you're carrying the first grandbaby in there," my mom said as she wiped at her eyes even though there were no tears falling.

"Oh jeez, Mom. You can't cry every time you talk about the baby," I complained. "Plus, she's going to be my best friend, so you can just step aside."

"I thought I was your best friend," Saint interrupted, and I leaned over to press a kiss to his mouth. "You are, sweetie. But she's going to be my new best girlfriend."

"I thought I was your best girlfriend." Cori's voice rang out from somewhere in the house, and without warning, she was suddenly in the room.

"What are you doing here?"

"Claiming my rightful place as best friend, obviously," she said with sass, her hair a peach color now, which, of course, flattered her.

I was still confused as to why Cori was in the house

during dinner when I heard Sam gasp. I shot her a look and realized that she wasn't looking at me, but at something on the floor. Thinking that there might be a giant spider or some kind of bug, I quickly looked in the direction she was, only to see Saint on one knee, holding a black velvet box in his hand.

HE. WAS. ON. ONE. KNEE.

And not because he was apologizing, if you get what I mean.

He opened the box slowly, revealing an enormous pear-shaped diamond inside, and my eyes felt like they might pop right out of their sockets at how wide they'd grown.

"Ivy Simpson," Saint said, and I focused all of my attention on him, his blue eyes shining, those two dimples tormenting me with their utter perfection.

He cleared his throat and started again. "Ivy Simpson, I've been in love with you since I was seventeen years old. Some jerk made me promise never to touch you, so I tried my best to stay away. But you can't keep a man from his destiny, his other half, his soul mate. And that's what you are to me. What you'll always be. Hell, I wanted to do this the day after we officially got together. Went out and bought you this ring two days later. I knew what I wanted that first night. What I'll always want every night from now until I die. You. Only you. There has never been and will never be another woman on this planet meant for me. Please say that you'll marry me. Say yes today and every day after it."

Saint had turned into a blurry blob, and I could barely see him through all my tears.

"Yes. Of course, yes. Always yes."

I still couldn't see him clearly as I felt him push the ring onto my finger, stopping slightly at the knuckle before forcing it over. It was a perfect fit. I should have known. Everything Saint did seemed to be. At least when it came to us.

His mouth was on mine, his tongue in my mouth, and I heard my brother make a gagging sound, but I couldn't care less. He had a head; he could turn it around and not watch.

When we broke the kiss, Saint wiped the tears from my eyes and cheeks. "I love you."

"I love you too."

"You're going to be my wife."

"I know!"

"Congratulations, bestie," Cori said, and I turned to hug her.

"Is that why you're here?"

"Of course. Saint would never propose in front of everyone and leave me out. I mean, he might have, but he would have paid for his insolence," she explained with a finger gesture, and I couldn't help but laugh. "Let me see that thing."

When I shoved my left hand in her face, she took it and let out a whistle. "Apparently, your man knows how you like things. BIG and MONSTER-SIZED!" she shouted, and I caught her double meaning before failing to shush her.

Saint might never forgive me if he knew I'd told Cori about his monster penis.

"Did you all know?" I looked around at everyone I considered family and watched them all nod their heads in unison.

They'd known this was happening today. They'd all seen the ring already. Saint had planned the entire thing.

"I wasn't going to ask you until dessert, but Cori's bitterness at losing best-friend status pushed it up a bit," Saint said loud enough for Cori to hear, but she only offered a one-shouldered shrug.

"I couldn't help it." She sounded so sincere that everyone consoled her, telling her that no little baby could ever replace her.

"I don't care," I shouted before hoisting my left hand toward the ceiling "I'm getting married!"

The room burst into cheers as my mom started pouring glasses of champagne for everyone, except Sam, who made a face like it wasn't fair.

"I'm sure one sip wouldn't hurt the baby. People used to drink and smoke while they were pregnant, and their kids were fine," Samantha said.

"I'm not sure that's true," I argued, and she shot me a death stare, so I shut my mouth.

Pregnant women were scary sometimes.

"To Saint and Ivy." My dad started making a toast as he held his glass in the air, and we all followed suit. "For finally getting it together and doing the one thing we all knew they'd do eventually. Thanks for putting us out of our misery."

"Amen to that!" Saint's dad agreed, and my mouth dropped open before I started to take a sip from my glass.

"Now, give us all the babies," my mom shouted, and everyone looked at her and busted out laughing.

I almost spit my liquid right out.

"Time to take away Mom's champagne," Davey said as he reached across the table for it, but she downed it in one gulp instead.

"Too slow," she mocked, and Davey shot me a look that said Mom was going to be a handful later.

Not our problem, I mouthed and gave a nod toward Dad.

He gave me a thumbs-up.

"Do you like the ring?" Saint's hot breath was in my ear, his words sending a shiver down my spine.

"It's stunning, but you could have given me a Ring Pop, and I still would have said yes."

I turned to face him as his arms wrapped around my middle, and he tugged me against his hard body.

"Now you tell me," he teased. "By the way, I need to take you home and have my way with you."

"We haven't even eaten dinner yet." I pouted a little because I was actually starving. I'd waited all day to eat this meal. Heck, I looked forward to it all year long.

"As soon as we eat, we leave," he demanded, and I touched his nose with my fingertip before pressing a kiss there.

"Fine." I acquiesced before I started imagining all the ways in which Saint might show me how much he loved and appreciated me.

We were engaged, and for whatever reason, I felt different even though nothing had technically changed. I just felt … *more*. More love for Saint. More emotional toward him. More secure. More confident.

"Make sure you bring some dessert home. I have plans for that whipped cream," he informed me as he wagged his eyebrows before shooting my private parts a glance.

The man was an absolute god in the bedroom. He hadn't stopped teaching me things since we'd started having sex. I hadn't known that it could be fun, comfortable, and so soul-connecting, all at once. I felt like I still had so much to learn. But I was nothing if not a willing student.

I'd thought last Christmas was the happiest I'd ever been. The time when Saint admitted his feelings for me and we finally got to become the couple I'd always wished for.

But this Christmas had far surpassed the last one. All because of one question and the ring on my finger.

I wondered what he'd do next Christmas.

The End

Thank you so much for reading. I hope you enjoyed Saint and Ivy's story. This one was such a blast for me and I had the best time writing it. I hope it was fun to read!

Have you been loving my seasonal-themed stories? Well, guess what! MORE ARE COMING! You'll have an ENTIRE YEAR'S worth of reads, starting in 2023. That's twelve stories- one a month- for a whole year!

Don't miss out on a single one. Make sure you join my NEWSLETTER (you can sign up on my website) today and get the details right in your inbox!

Other Books by J. Sterling

Bitter Rivals—an enemies-to-lovers romance
Dear Heart, I Hate You
In Dreams—a new adult college romance
Chance Encounters—a coming-of-age story

THE GAME SERIES
The Perfect Game—Book One
The Game Changer—Book Two
The Sweetest Game—Book Three
The Other Game (Dean Carter)—Book Four

THE PLAYBOY SERIAL
Avoiding the Playboy—Episode #1
Resisting the Playboy—Episode #2
Wanting the Playboy—Episode #3

THE CELEBRITY SERIES
Seeing Stars—Madison & Walker
Breaking Stars—Paige & Tatum
Losing Stars—Quinn & Ryson

THE FISHER BROTHERS SERIES
No Bad Days—a new adult, second-chance romance
Guy Hater—an emotional love story

Adios Pantalones—a single-mom romance
Happy Ending

THE BOYS OF BASEBALL
(THE NEXT GENERATION OF FULLTON STATE BASEBALL
PLAYERS)
The Ninth Inning—Cole Anders
Behind the Plate—Chance Carter
Safe at First—Mac Davies

FUN FOR THE HOLIDAYS
(A COLLECTION OF STAND-ALONE NOVELS WITH HOLIDAY-
BASED THEMES)
Kissing My Coworker
Dumped for Valentine's
My Week with the Prince
Fools in Love
Spring's Second Chance
Don't Marry Him
Summer Lovin'
Soaring Through August
Falling for the Boss
Tricked by My Ex
The Thanksgiving Hookup
Christmas with Saint

About the Author

Jenn Sterling is a Southern California native who loves writing stories from the heart. Every story she tells has pieces of her truth in it as well as her life experience. She has her bachelor's degree in radio/TV/film and has worked in the entertainment industry the majority of her life.

Jenn loves hearing from her readers and can be found online at:

Blog & Website:
www.j-sterling.com

Twitter:
www.twitter.com/AuthorJSterling

Facebook:
www.facebook.com/AuthorJSterling

Instagram & TikTok:
@ AuthorJSterling

If you enjoyed this book, please consider writing a spoiler-free review on the site from which you purchased it. And thank you so much for helping me spread the word about my books and for allowing me to continue telling the stories I love to tell. I appreciate you so much. :)

Thank you for purchasing this book.

Come join my private reader group on Facebook for giveaways:

PRIVATE READER GROUP

facebook.com/groups/ThePerfectGameChangerGroup

Made in the USA
Middletown, DE
22 September 2022

10690435R00078